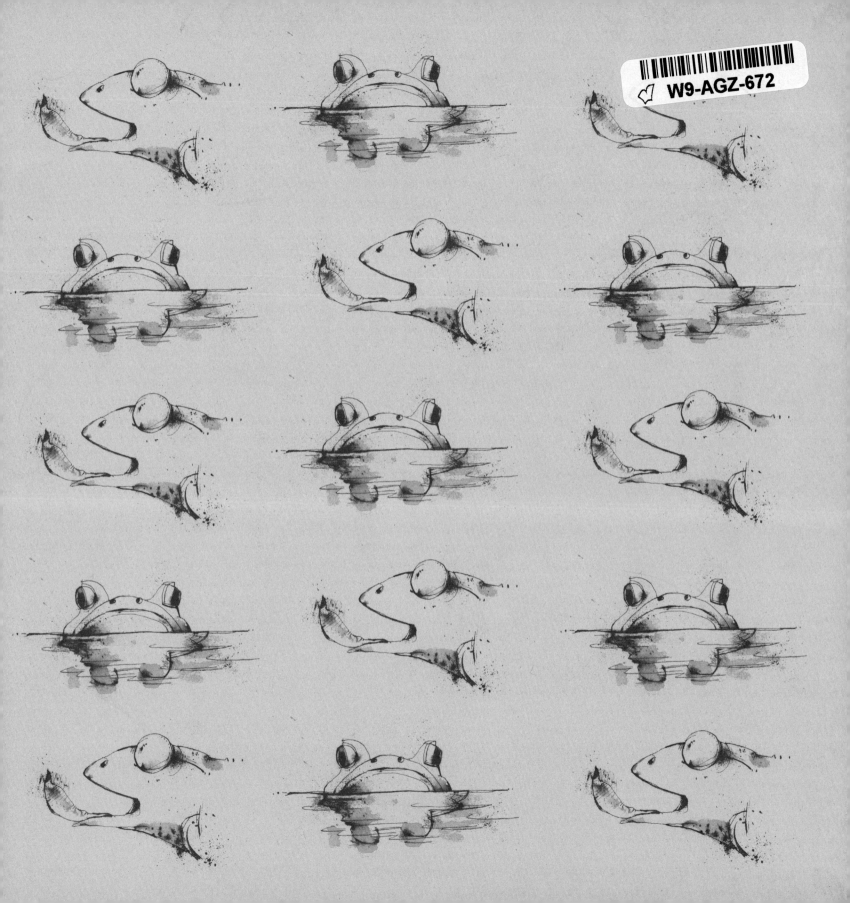

Dear Mark,

Happy Birthday! You are 5 years old — how big you are getting and how proud we are of you.

Maybe you'll enjoy reading about frogs, but aren't you glad you aren't a frog!

We love you,
Uncle Bud & Aunt Tomi

It's a
Frog's Life

If found, please return this journal to:

NAME	Frog
ADDRESS	The Pond
AGE	5 years old
COLORING	Mottled greenish-brown

Favorite things:

FOOD	Flies, slugs, and beetles
PLACES	Cool, muddy places
TIME OF YEAR	Spring

Reader's Digest Children's Books
are published by Reader's Digest Children's Publishing, Inc.
Reader's Digest Road, Pleasantville, NY 10570-7000

Conceived, edited, and designed by Tucker Slingsby Limited
Berkeley House, 73 Upper Richmond Road, London SW15 2SZ

Illustrations by Robert Morton, Robin Carter, and Philip Bishop
Text by Steve Parker and Frog

Library of Congress Cataloging-in-Publication Data
Parker, Steve.
It's a Frog's Life/ with the help of Steve Parker;
[illustrations by Robert Morton, Robin Carter, and Philip Bishop].
p. cm.
Summary: Uses the viewpoint of a frog to present life at a busy English pond,
including the activities of other frogs, a toad, a newt, and a heron.
ISBN 1-57584-250-5 (hc.)
1. Frogs—Juvenile literature. 2. Pond ecology—juvenile literature. [1. Frogs. 2. Pond ecology. 3. Ecology.]
I. Morton, Robert, ill. II. Carter, Robin, ill. III. Bishop, Philip, ill. IV. Title.
QL668.E2P297 1999
597.8'9—dc21 98-38271

It's a
Frog's Life

by Frog, with help from

Steve Parker

Reader's Digest Children's Books™
Pleasantville, New York * Montreal, Canada

ME—EATING A TASTY SNACK

ALL ABOUT ME

Well, here we go—the first page of my very own journal. I've always wanted to keep one, and this year I'm going to do it. I'll call it "A Year in the Life of an Observant Frog!"

I'm feeling pretty stiff and slow today. I'm also very hungry! It's not surprising—I've been asleep for, well, months! The whole winter, in fact.

It's still not very warm yet, and I'm kind of slow when it's cold. So today I'll just do a few stretching exercises. I can start looking for food tomorrow, when I'm warmer and I can move faster.

LAST YEAR AT THE POND—I'M ON THE LILY PAD!

I think I should start this journal with a few notes about me. I'm a frog. I've got two big eyes to see my food with and one wide mouth to gulp it down. I've got a tubby green body, two strong back legs for leaping, and two small front legs for landing on—but no tail. Know-it-all Newt told me I'm an amphibian. He gave me this piece of paper out of a book to explain what being an amphibian means. He's one, too!

When it's warm enough, I live near the Pond. It's a busy place. There are ducks, fish, and bugs, as well as lots of other frogs, and visitors from far away. Life is never dull. There's always someone to catch for lunch!

MY DRAWING OF NEWT

All About Amphibians
(say "am-fib-ee-ans")

• Amphibians are one of the main groups of vertebrates—animals with backbones. The others are fish, reptiles, birds, and mammals.
• There are about 4,000 kinds, or species, of amphibians.
• Amphibians live all around the world, except in cold polar lands or in the sea. Most prefer lakes, streams, and damp places, but some like deserts!
• Amphibians are cold-blooded. This means that their bodies are the same temperature as their surroundings. Cold weather slows them down. Warm weather heats their blood, which makes them active.
• There are three main groups of amphibians:

1. **Newts and salamanders**
Creatures in this group have tails.

2. **Frogs and toads**
These animals have no tails.

3. **Caecilians**
These legless, tailless amphibians look like big earthworms. They live mainly in the soil of tropical forests.

HOORAY! IT'S SPRING

At last! Sunshine in my den. This is where I sleep all winter. Newt says our winter sleep is called hibernation. All I know is that I've been too cold to move anywhere. Now I'm warming up. Tomorrow I plan to hop over the log, through the marsh, across the road (the dangerous part), and on to my favorite place—the Pond. Newt's coming, too.

I'm STARVING—I haven't eaten for five months! But I've got to get to the Pond right away, and I don't want to waste time looking for food here. I'll have to gulp down a meal or two along the way.

DRAWINGS OF WHAT I WANT TO EAT TOMORROW!

BEETLES—crunchy outside, soft and tasty inside. Yum, yum!

SLUGS—slow and slippery. They slide down in one swallow!

I picked this snowdrop to show that spring is almost here. But flowers aren't frog food.

Late Summer   Early Fall   Late Fall   Winter

BACK TO THE POND

The trip to the Pond took forever—two days, in fact! I'm small and slow, and I have to keep hiding from creatures that want to EAT ME! And I have to stay out of the sun, which can dry me out.

First I waddled along, then took a rest. After a small hop or two more, it was time to rest again. It would be quicker if I took big leaps, but they're so tiring! Leaps are great for escaping from danger but no good on a long journey like this.

I had to watch out for danger every hop of the way. Then, just after one long waddle and a small jump, I paused. Or should I say PAWS! There in front of me was Cat! I took one big leap and another and—phew!—I was back at the Pond with my friends! Was I glad THAT was over.

Oops! ANOTHER MUDDY PRINT!

It was great to see the usual crowd at the Pond. Some of them, like Toad, are as slow as me. But Duck, Mouse—and of course the horrible Cat—move faster. They always seem to be warm. I think it's something to do with their blood. Newt says they're warm-blooded.

MY AMAZING LEAP AWAY FROM DANGER!

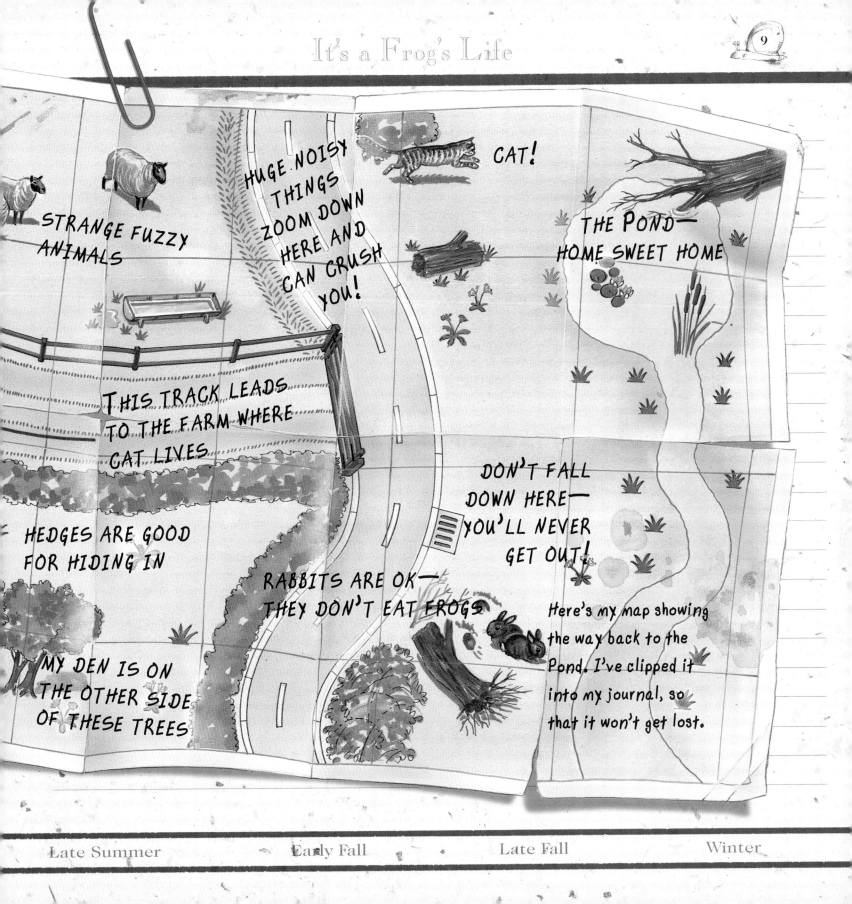

HOME SWEET HOME

If you ask me, the Pond is PERFECT.
There's lots of cool water to swim in and
keep my skin moist. The banks are nice
and muddy and damp. The plants are big
enough to give me shade and to hide in.
And there are lots of small creatures to
catch and eat. YUMMY!

Best of all, there are lots of other frogs.
For most of the year I keep to myself, but
in the spring we frogs all get together to
breed. Must keep the species going.

Today, once I found a comfortable muddy
spot, I checked out the Pond for danger.
I ALWAYS do that! It was full of crystal
clear water—not murky and almost dried
out, like last year. But then I
spotted the tracks of a
strange animal...

MY DRAWING OF THE STRANGE FOOTPRINT

Early Spring   Late Spring   Early Summer

You've got to be something of a nature detective to survive in the wild! Animals walk across the soft mud and leave tracks. Most I already know. Some tracks don't worry me, like Squirrel and Deer. Others—especially Gull, Badger, and Heron—spell D-A-N-G-E-R!

I've never seen anything like the footprints I found today. I thought this page—from a book I found by the Pond—would help, but the stranger's feet aren't in there.

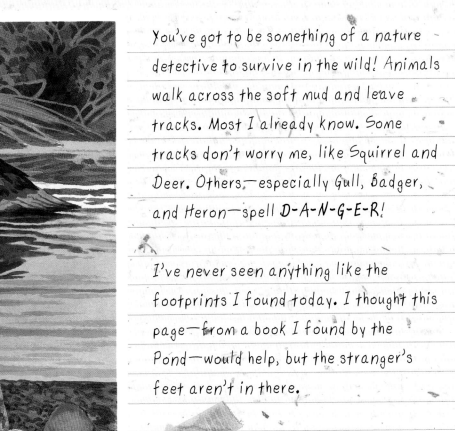

Animal Tracks

Squirrel Badger Fallow Deer

Gull Heron

WURP, RIBBIT, CROAK!

What a noisy few days it's been! My froggy friends are swimming and splashing, calling and croaking. It's always like this in the early spring because it's our breeding season.

All the male frogs, including me, start by croaking and calling to the female frogs. We make our loud croaks by sucking in air and blowing it out. This makes our throats swell up like **BALLOONS**!

When the females hear the noise, they join us in the Pond. Frogs don't have big ears that stick up like Rabbit's, but our hearing is just as good. Anyway, we males make so much noise, the females can't miss it!

Then we all push and shove, trying to find a good partner. Eventually everyone finds a mate. Each male frog holds on to his female, sometimes for two or three days!

The females lay their eggs in the water. Each egg is a tiny black dot covered with jelly. The males then lay their sperm over the eggs.

I don't really understand this part, but Know-it-all Newt says that each egg has to combine with a sperm before it can grow into a baby frog. Newt calls this "fertilization."

All I know is that the Pond is full to the brim with slippery, jelly-covered eggs. Some of us call the eggs "frog spawn."

ME AND MY FRIENDS SOUNDING OFF

THAT'S ME—CROAKING AT THE TOP OF MY LUNGS!

Early Spring   Late Spring   Early Summer

EGGS OVER EASY

Today, I had it out with Newt. He's an **EGG-STEALER!** Newt thinks frog spawn is snack food. So do some of the other animals in the Pond. Water beetles, dragonfly nymphs, and fish all help themselves to our eggs!

Frog eggs might be tasty but to actually eat them—UGH! Of course, frogs do lay lots of eggs. It's a good thing, too!

Each female frog can lay about 2,000 eggs in a big clump. Toads lay about the same number, but in a long rope, like a necklace, that's wound around underwater leaves and stems. Newt eggs are kind of like frog eggs, but smaller. And each one is laid separately, usually under a leaf.

If you think about it, the Pond would be pretty crowded if all the eggs hatched and the babies survived to adulthood. Hmmm. Perhaps it's just as well so many get eaten!

I've noticed that different animals have very different eggs. Here are some of the things I've spotted:

• Pond Snail's eggs are like ours—covered with jelly—but they are **MUCH** smaller. They are laid in a strip on an underwater leaf.

• Moorhen's eggs are huge! They have a hard outside shell instead of jelly. This is OK because they are **NOT IN WATER** at all! Amazing! They're outside, in the air. Without a hard shell, they'd shrivel and dry up. You know, all the birds seem to lay hard-shelled eggs. Sometimes the empty shells fall into the water from their nests.

MOORHEN

MORE SHELLS I'VE COLLECTED

THESE BELONG TO OTHER BIRDS

MOORHEN'S EGG

Late Summer   Early Fall   Late Fall   Winter

LITTLE WRIGGLERS

It's now the middle of spring, and I've been too busy to write in my journal for a while. Every day is warmer— and more crowded! Our eggs have hatched into tiny tadpoles—I call them wrigglers because wriggle is just what they do!

Jelly babies

This picture shows the tiny frog babies before they've hatched. They float in their jelly covering for around two weeks before wriggling free. I like them at this stage. They're no trouble! But hungry fish (and newts!) are a problem...

Eating machines

As soon as they've hatched, the little rascals eat almost anything they can find—even bits of rotting plants and animals. They're funny-looking little things—all tail and no legs. Just the opposite of me!

Tadpole Timetable

Week 1   2,000 eggs laid
Week 3   1,000 baby tadpoles hatched
Week 5   Less than 500 tadpoles left— many are eaten by pond creatures and birds
Week 7   200 tadpoles with back legs
Week 10   Now 100 tadpoles, with their tails starting to shrink
Week 12   25 tadpoles left and now they have front legs, too.
Week 15   Only 10 are left. But they are no longer tadpoles—they are froglets!

Early Spring   Late Spring   Early Summer

Time for legs

About seven weeks after hatching, the babies start to grow back legs and learn to swim by kicking them in the water. I call this the froggy paddle!

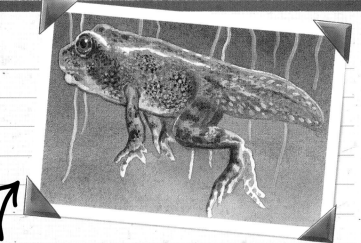

More legs and less tail!

About five weeks after the froggy paddle stage, the tadpoles' front legs pop out and their tails began to shrink. There's no stopping them now—they can breathe out of water by gulping air into their lungs. Before, they had gills to breathe with underwater.

My favorite froglet

This is one of my favorite daughters, 15 weeks after hatching. To look at her now, sitting on MY lily pad, you'd never guess that she was once an egg and a wriggly little tadpole. Newt, who knows long words (and how to spell them), says that this change in shape is called "metamorphosis." All frogs (and newts) do it!

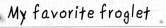

Late Summer   Early Fall   Late Fall   Winter

HUNGRY ALL THE TIME

Whrrrr. A big—and I mean *BIG*—dragonfly whizzed past me today and landed on a leaf. I was hungry, and dragonflies are very tasty. Some are so big that if I catch them, I don't have to eat again for days! But they're strong, too. They can give you nasty jabs with the sharp claws on their feet.

I catch small flies by flicking out my tongue and *SNAP*—they're stuck on its sticky tip. This monster looked too big for that, so I went for the bold approach. I leaped up and grabbed it in my fabulously wide mouth. Let me tell you—that leap was *INCREDIBLE!*

It was kind of a struggle to swallow the dragonfly, but I got it down in the end. It was the best meal I've had in a long time.

THIS IS MY DRAWING OF MY LONG, STICKY TONGUE!

Fast food . . .

I only eat living animals.
Nothing dead—UGH!
Butterflies are pretty—
and pretty tasty!

Flies are yummy, too. So
are bees. Bees get so busy
collecting pollen from
flowers that they don't
notice me creeping up!

. . . and slow food!

Snails are terrific! So
slow and easy to
catch! I scrunch them
up and spit out the
pieces of shell.

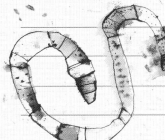

Frogs have no teeth so
we slurp up worms whole.
They wriggle all the way
down. Dee-licious!

THE SCARY PART

Today was a **BAD DAY**! Heron visited the Pond. I haven't been so frightened since I saw Fox last winter. I was sitting at the edge of the water when I felt the telltale ripples. I dived away just in time. A huge foot landed EXACTLY where I had been sitting!

I kept very still. My greenish-brown skin matches the mud and stones. If I don't move, I'm almost invisible. At least, I've lived through five summers, so it must work.

Nothing happened for a long time. A few other pond animals began to move. But I could still see the shadow of that big leg, so I stayed **VERY, VERY STILL**. Then suddenly— SPLASH! A sharp beak stabbed through the water. I was absolutely terrified. That beak was bigger than me!

A FEATHER THAT
HERON LEFT BEHIND

It was Heron! I actually saw his head and his big, beady eyes. He grabbed a fish in his beak, threw it high into the air, and GULP! Then the water swirled and the great bird flapped his wings and was gone. The danger was over.

Many creatures try to eat us frogs. We have to watch out for lots of birds. Besides herons, there are gulls and grebes at the Pond, and crows and magpies hopping along the banks. I've seen frogs caught by cats, rats, foxes, hedgehogs, and grass snakes. Cats are the worst—they watch us for hours and then slash through the water with razor-sharp claws. SCARY!

Daily Clarion

Vanishing Pond Life

If you value the frogs, newts, and fish in your pond, cover it with a net! Frogs and other water creatures are being caught and killed at an alarming rate. Herons are often blamed for emptying a pond, but your cat may be the real culprit.

SUMMER NIGHTS

I don't do much except eat during the long summer days. I have a "see-food" diet—if I see food, I eat it! Otherwise, I just sit around and relax. Some animals are so busy, rushing around, always doing something. It makes me tired just to look at them.

During the night, I do even less. Darkness is so-oo-oo spooky! By day, my huge eyes can spot tiny gnats and midges flitting past. But at night, I can't see as well. So I find a safe place, keep my eyes open, and wait until daylight. If the moon is bright, I can see animals moving around. The moon was out last night, so I was able to record these events.

MOTHS LIKE THIS ARE ALWAYS FLUTTERING AROUND AT NIGHT

NATURE NOTES—BY FROG

Written by the light of Glowworm and her friends. (Glowworm says they're not really worms. They're female fireflies that can't fly. They glow to attract a mate. I've taped in a picture to show what they look like.)

SKY—Bat is flitting around. Bat is like a bird, but has fur instead of feathers. Bat is always chasing moths. Why? Maybe to catch and eat, like I catch flies.

NEAR—I caught a caterpillar and swallowed it whole. I saw Mouse eat one, too, so there must be a shortage of her usual seeds, nuts, and berries. Land Snail slowly slides up a stem, looking for juicy leaves to eat. Snails certainly live life in the slow lane!

FAR—In a distant field, I can just see deer nibbling at leaves. I know about deer because they come to the Pond to drink and leave their footprints in the mud.

OH, NO! THERE'S WEASEL! Mouse is in trouble. Come to think of it, a hungry weasel might even eat me! Gotta go!

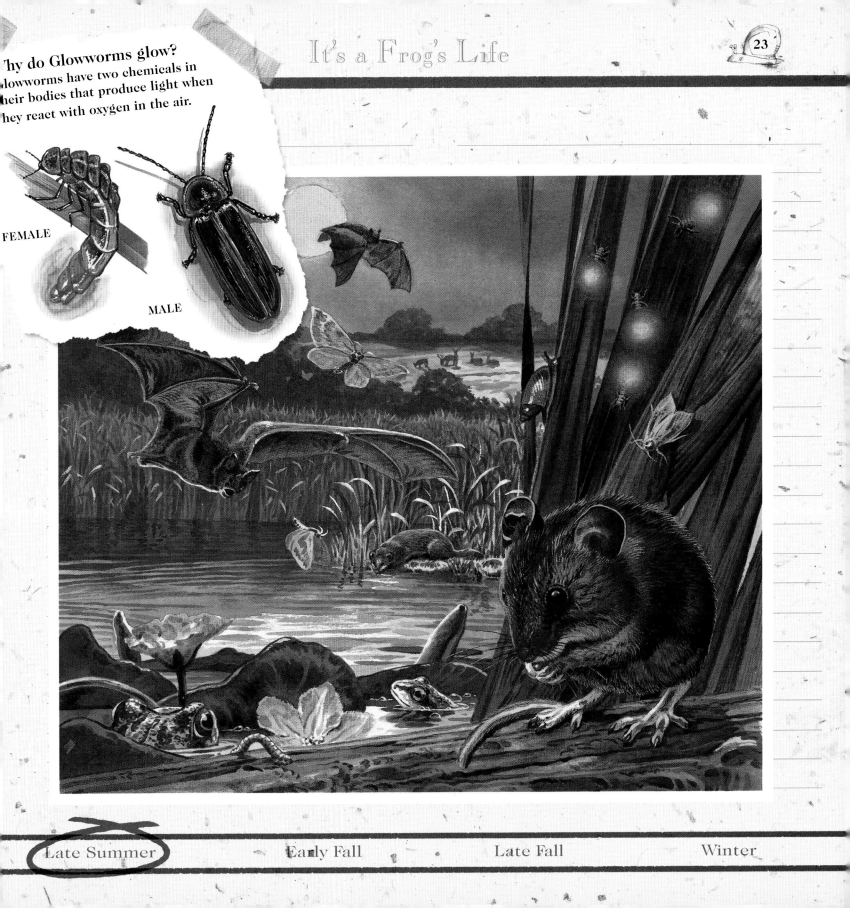

Why do Glowworms glow?
Glowworms have two chemicals in their bodies that produce light when they react with oxygen in the air.

FEMALE

MALE

DRY IS DANGEROUS

PHEW! IT'S HOT! I may be cold-blooded, but today my blood must be hotter than Mouse's! I can only stay in the sun for a few minutes before my skin starts to feel dry and stiff. If I don't hide in the water or under a cool, damp stone, I could dry out and **DIE!**

The Pond always gets smaller in the summer when the sun's hot and the days are long. But it's even worse than last year. It hasn't rained for **WEEKS.**

Luckily, I don't have to live in water all the time like Fish does. I can live in water and on land, as long as the land is damp. That's because I'm an amphibian. Newt says this word means "alternate lives" and that means I can live in two kinds of places. Newt sure is a know-it-all!

In fact, my friends and I don't stay in the Pond for long. Sure, we go there in early spring to breed. But by early summer, we move to nearby patches of damp undergrowth, bushes, and shady plants. Our amphibian cousins Toad and Newt do the same.

If it doesn't rain soon, the Pond will disappear completely. So will Fish and his friends.

LOVE THOSE LILY PADS! GREAT TO SIT ON—OR HIDE UNDER.

TIME TO LEAVE

Today summer has turned to fall. The sun is weaker, the days are shorter, and the raindrops are bigger. It's good to feel the rain, but the wet is chilly now. It cools my body down, and I can't move as quickly.

The rain has filled up the Pond—everywhere is nice and damp. I like the wet grass and leaves, but Sparrow and Shrew are shivering. There aren't so many flies and other things for me to catch. They must go away for the winter, too.

Everything's changing. Leaves are turning brown and falling off the trees. Seeds, berries, and nuts grow in their place. Mouse and Vole love them. I tried a blackberry once. YUCK! It didn't wriggle, and it didn't taste like meat. Frogs are NOT plant eaters!

NOW ONE'S FALLEN ON MY PAGE! WHAT A MESS!

It will soon be time for my winter sleep. I'll turn back to my map (I knew this journal would come in handy!). It will show me the way back to my winter den.

Good-bye, Pond—until next year!

SNACKS TO EAT ON THE WAY BACK—

SPIDER has lots of wriggly legs and a hairy body, but is soft and juicy inside.

CRANE FLY is very spindly. I can hardly taste the thin legs and wings. They snap off at my first bite!

BUSH CRICKET has strong back legs that kick hard, like mine. Oooh—my mouth!

DUNG FLY—I'm not sure what "dung" is, but this fly is extra juicy and extra sweet. Yummy!

BACK TO SLEEP

I almost didn't make it back to my den. I saw more of those strange footprints I first spotted by the Pond last spring. Then I saw the creature who made them—MINK! She's worse than Heron and just as bad as Cat! She swims as well as I do, and eats water animals—fish, newts, and frogs!

I hid until Mink was gone. I was almost too cold to move, but I knew I had to keep going.

I reached my den at last. It was nearly dark. I hopped along the track, through the trees, and found my hidey-hole just as I left it. I'm lucky it was still there. Last year, Toad went back to her usual winter den, but it was gone. No trees or bushes. Just a huge, flat, stinky blackness, and spinning things that can crush you flat.

ACORN—SQUIRREL'S FAVORITE FOOD

OAK LEAF

This is my last entry in my very first journal. Soon I'll bury myself in leaves, moss, and soil, safe from frosts and predators— that's another word Newt taught me. It's been a great year! I've learned so much AND I've lived to write about it! Few frogs reach such a ripe old age. Next spring I'll be six.

When it's warm again, I think I'll start another journal. I want to draw some more pictures, too. But now, it's time to settle down. I'll just take a last look at the cards and photos my relatives have sent me this year. I've pasted them in on the next page.

MY FROGGY FRIENDS

These frogs are some of my friends and relatives. They look different from me because they live in far-off places.

They sometimes send me postcards, photos, and letters. I always write back to them—they like to hear about life in the Pond, and I do little drawings for them, too!

BEADY

He's a red-eyed tree frog. Beady lives in a warm, wet, tropical forest in Costa Rica. That's in Central America—it takes forever for his postcards to arrive! Beady's small, but he has huge eyes so he can see in the dark forest. He's got sticky pads on his toes for holding on to slippery leaves and branches. I'd like to visit Beady—a warm, damp forest sounds good to me!

SHEILA

This is my friend, a water-holding frog from Australia. She lives in a place that sounds awful to me—a DRY DESERT! She hides underground for months, in a kind of wet sleeping bag made from her own body water. Sometimes thirsty humans dig her up and try to squeeze the water out of her for a drink. UGH!

GREEDY

These are my favorite photos! Greedy's a bush squeaker from Africa. Greedy says her part of Africa is very hot, so she has to be extra careful about getting too much sun (dry skin can be deadly to us frogs!). Greedy tells me there are LOTS of flies in Africa, so she sent me these pictures of her catching one. Hunh! I can do that tongue trick, too!

TUBS

This is one cousin I don't want to meet! Tubs is an American Bullfrog. He is one of the biggest frogs in the world. Bullfrogs eat lots of animals, including rats, lizards and even other frogs, like me. GULP!

SMARTY

All us frogs have skin that tastes bad. That often keeps birds from eating us. But Smarty's a poison dart frog from South America—his skin can kill a predator! He says his bright blue color warns animals to stay away.

Late Summer   Early Fall   Fall   Winter

DIFFICULT WORDS I'VE LEARNED FROM KNOW-IT-ALL NEWT

AMPHIBIAN
A creature that can live in water and on land (like me!).

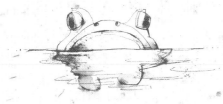

COLD-BLOODED
When an animal is the same temperature as its surroundings, hot in summer and cold in winter (also like me!).

DUNG
Newt says this is waste stuff that comes out of your rear end. Deer make mountains of it near the Pond!

EGG
A tiny blob that grows into a baby. We all started as one (even readers of my journal).

FISH
An animal that has gills to breathe with, a scaly body, fins, and a tail. It always lives in the water.

FERTILIZATION
When an egg from a female combines with a sperm from a male and starts to grow into a baby.

FROG SPAWN
A jumble of eggs from a female frog. They're covered in slimy, see-through jelly.

HIBERNATION
When a creature falls deep asleep, usually in winter. Newt says we do this. I'm too cold and tired to remember.

MAMMAL
A warm-blooded creature (like Cat) who's always ready for action—and covered in fur or hair, not in moist skin or scales.

METAMORPHOSIS
The way some creatures change shape as they grow up. I did this, from tadpole to me. So did Moth, who was once a caterpillar.

NYMPH
A young insect that lives in water and looks different from a grown-up. Dragonfly was once a nymph.

PREDATORS
Animals that eat other animals, like Cat and Heron. Newt says I'm a predator, too, because I eat flies and worms.

REPTILE
A cold-blooded animal, like me, but covered in strong scales (not moist skin). Snake, Lizard, and Tortoise are reptiles.

SPERM
A teeny tiny tadpole-like thing that combines with an egg to make a baby.

TROPICAL
What you call a place that's warm all year. It's a long way from here—even farther than to the Pond and back.

WARM-BLOODED
An animal that makes its own body heat and is warm all the time (like Cat!). Only mammals and birds do this.